My Storytime

Jack Digger
Helps Out

written by Nicola Baxter
illustrated by Alex Burnett

Bright and early one morning, Jack Digger went to a big green field.

"I've got a very important job for you," said the workman, looking at a huge piece of paper. "We need to dig a hole right here."

6

"When there's digging to be done, I'm the digger to do it!" said Jack Digger. "But can you tell me what…?"

"Sorry," the man with the plan interrupted. "I'll have a word with you later. I'm just nipping off for some breakfast."

7

So, with a *clank, clankety clank,* Jack Digger started to dig. Soon he had made a neat round hole and a little pile of earth and grass.

Along came Mrs Macgregor and her little girl Maisy on their way to the shops. "What are you digging?" asked Mrs Macgregor.

"Err… I don't know yet," said Jack Digger.

"I do!" said Maisy. "It's a hole for a Giant Flopsy Hopsy Bunny. We'll come back later to see it."

Mrs Macgregor and Maisy went on their way and the man with the plan came back from his breakfast. He looked at the little round hole and shook his head.

"I'm afraid", he said, "that the hole needs to be oblong, not round. Keep digging, Jack Digger!"

"That's what I do best!" said Jack Digger.
"But I wonder if you could tell me…?"

But the man with the plan had gone off
for a cup of coffee and a look at his
newspaper.

So Jack Digger started work again. With a *clank, clankety clank,* he made the sides of the hole steep and straight. The pile of earth grew as big as a lorry.

Along came Barry, Harry and Gary on their way to school. "What are you digging?" they asked.

"Err..." said Jack Digger, "I'm not allowed to say what it is quite yet."

"I bet I know," said Barry. "It's a pond for a fierce digger-crunching Shinkle Shark. We'll come back after school to see it."

Barry, Harry and Gary went off to school and the man with the plan came back from his coffee break. He looked carefully at the hole and shook his head.

"It's the right shape," he said, "but it needs to be a lot bigger! Keep digging!"

"No problem!" said Jack Digger. "Can you tell me…?"

"You're doing a good job! Keep it up!" said the man with the plan, looking at his watch. "I'll be back after lunch."

So, with a *clank, clankety clank,* Jack Digger started work again. The oblong hole got bigger and bigger and the pile of earth and grass grew as high as a house.

Along came Daisy and Jim with their dog, Tickles. "What is this big oblong hole for?" they asked. "Come here, Tickles!"

"Err, I'm afraid that's top secret," said Jack Digger. "I really can't say."

"It looks to me as though it might be a trap for a Many-headed Monster," said Jim. "I saw one once on the telly…"

"I don't think so, Jim," said Daisy. "We'll come back later to see."

18

Daisy, Jim and Tickles went on their way and the man with the plan came back from his lunch. He measured all around the hole. Then he shook his head.

"It's the right size now," he said, "but it needs to be much deeper – especially this end! Keep digging, Jack Digger!"

"No sooner said than done!" said Jack Digger. "Could you…?"

But the man with the plan had gone off to have a little snooze.

So, with a *clank, clankety clank*, Jack Digger started work again. The hole got deeper and deeper and the pile of earth grew as high as a hill.

Along came Sophie and her bicycle, training for a race. "What are you digging?" she asked.

"Well…" began Jack Digger. But Sophie was already pedalling up the pile of earth.

"Don't tell me, I've guessed!" she puffed.
"It's for my hill-climbing practice! I'll be
back to try it again later."

Sophie whizzed off and the man with the plan came back from his snooze. He smiled when he saw the hole.

"This is just right," he said. "But you haven't finished yet, Jack Digger. Look at all this earth. It needs to be carried to those lorries over there and taken away. You're the digger for the job! Keep digging!"

"Just leave it to me!" said Jack Digger.
"Does that mean…?"

But the man with the plan had gone off to
have a cup of tea.

So, with a *clank, clankety clank*, Jack Digger carried all the earth and all the grass over to the lorries. Some builders came and started work on the hole.

But no matter how much Jack Digger tried to peep, he couldn't see what they were doing.

Meanwhile, Mrs Macgregor and Maisy came back from the shops. Barry, Harry and Gary came out of school. Daisy, Jim and Tickles came past. And Sophie whizzed by on her bicycle. The man with the plan had a quiet word with all of them.

25

Just as Jack Digger put the very last scoop of soil into the very last lorry, the builders stopped work as well. Along came the man with – a great big smile!

"Now that I've finished…" began Jack Digger. But the man with the plan wasn't listening.

"There's one more very important job for you to do," he said. "Hold the end of this banner as high as you can."

With a *clank, clankety clank,* Jack Digger lifted the banner high above… the brand new swimming pool!

Splish! Splash! In jumped Mrs Macgregor and Maisy. *Splosh!* In jumped Harry, Barry and Gary.

In jumped Daisy and Jim and… oh no!
Stay there, Tickles! *Swoosh!* In dived
Sophie with hardly a splash. And look out!
Splat! In jumped the man – without
his plan!

"You kept this secret very well, Jack
Digger!" they called. Jack Digger just
gave them a big smile.